Levi the Lamb's Big Day

Written by **Aaron Carter**

Illustrated by **Anni Betts**

Powered by

PPL companies

Today is a Big Day for Levi the Lamb.
Levi and some of his lamb buddies
have been chosen to help save the
planet, and today is the day
he leaves for his big job.

"It's finally here!
Today's the Big Day
when I get to help out the planet
in a big, big way.
I wonder what I'll get to do?
Maybe my barnyard pals will have a clue ..."

"Percy, my piglet,
today's the Big Day!
I get to help save the planet,
I just don't know in what way."

Percy oinked:
"I don't know much about your Big Day,
but congrats, woo-hoo, and hooray!
Maybe today you'll blast off into space,
get rid of the pollution and clean up the place."

"Chester, my favorite chick,
it's my Big Day, woo-hoo!
I'm off to save the planet,
I wonder what I'll get to do?"

Chester peeped: "Oh, yay!
I'm so excited for your Big Day!
Maybe you'll go to the ocean floor
to save the sea turtles,
coral reefs, and more!"

"Franklin, you fair foal,
today's the Big Day!
I get to help save the planet,
I just don't know in what way."

"Giddy up!" said Franklin.
"It's your Big Day.
I hope it goes great
and you can still play.
Maybe you'll be up
in a windmill's cockpit
creating green energy
in your pilot's outfit."

"Kenzie, you clever calf,
  today's the Big Day!
  I get to help save the planet –
  I don't know how, but hooray!"

Kenzie mooed: "That's today?
Well, what do you say!?
Maybe you'll zip across
the rainforest canopy,
saving the Amazon
by planting more trees."

"Doris, you dashing donkey you,
today's the Big Day!
I get to help save the planet,
I just don't know in what way."

"It's today!?" Doris brayed.
"Hip, hip, hooray
for your big Big Day!
Maybe you'll be at the
hydro plant helping out,
surfing big waves and making
electricity, no doubt."

"Bella, you cool cat,
  it's my Big Day, oh wow!
  I get to help save the planet,
  I'm just not sure how."

"Right!" meowed Bella. "Great, okay!
We must prepare you for the Big Day.
Maybe you'll keep bees
at a pollinator habitat,
planting some flowers,
watching the hives and all that."

"Katie, my good kid,
today's the Big Day!
I get to help save the planet,
I just don't know in what way."

Katie bleated: "Hey, Levi, hey! Congrats on your Big Day!
Maybe you'll work in solar fields on the sun,
harvesting fresh sunlight, won't that be fun?"

"Well, I better get going.
I don't want to be late.
The first day on my dream job,
I just can't wait!"

Percy said: "C'mon, guys.
Let's go say goodbye.
We're gonna miss him a lot,
so it's okay to cry."

"Hello, lamb friends.
Today's our Big Day!
We get to help save the planet,
but does anyone know in what way?"

Robert The Ram chimed in:
"Dear Lambs, don't you know?
You're going to one of Kentucky's bigges
solar fields to mow."

"We get to save the planet
by eating grass with our friends?
That's the best I've heard yet,
I hope this job never ends!"

"Goodbye, my good barnyard friends.
The planet will be safe
when I see you again."

"Good luck!" oinked Percy.
"And have lots of fun!
We'll see you back here
when your big job is done!"

"I could get used to doing this every day.
Fresh grass in the sun is way better than hay.
I love helping the planet at home in Kentucky.
I can't help but think, we are so lucky!"

Levi's Big Day has come to an awesome end,
but his work to save the planet is just getting started.
We hope you're as excited to help the environment
as Levi and his lamb friends. Turn the page for some
fun projects you can do at home to help out.

Things You Can Do at Home to Help Levi the Lamb Help the Environment

We hope you enjoyed the story of Levi the Lamb and his Big Day. If you want to help Levi and his lamb friends out, you can do your part to help save the planet with these simple sustainability activities at home.

ride your bike

always turn the lights off when you leave a room

make your own laundry detergent

adjust the thermostat up or down 2 degrees in the summer and winter

wash your laundry in cold water

make a worm farm

check and change air filters

pick up trash around your neighborhood

grow a pollinator garden

compost your food scraps

install a water barrel

recycle paper and plastic

turn off the water when brushing your teeth

plant a tree

read more books about sustainability

Levi the Lamb's Big Day
Published by LG&E and KU Energy LLC with Scoppechio©
First Edition 2022
Text ©2022 by Aaron Carter
Illustrations ©2022 by Anni Betts
ISBN 979-8-9857607-0-5